VOLUME 18

JADE'S EROTIC ADVENTURES - BOOK 18

COPYRIGHT

The Therapist © 2019 Victoria Rush

Cover Design © 2019 PhotoMaras

Spying on the neighbors just got a lot more interesting...

Everything's sexier in the dark...

NUDE CRUISE

AN EROTIC ADVENTURE

VICTORIA RUSH

Some people get wet on a cruise for different reasons...

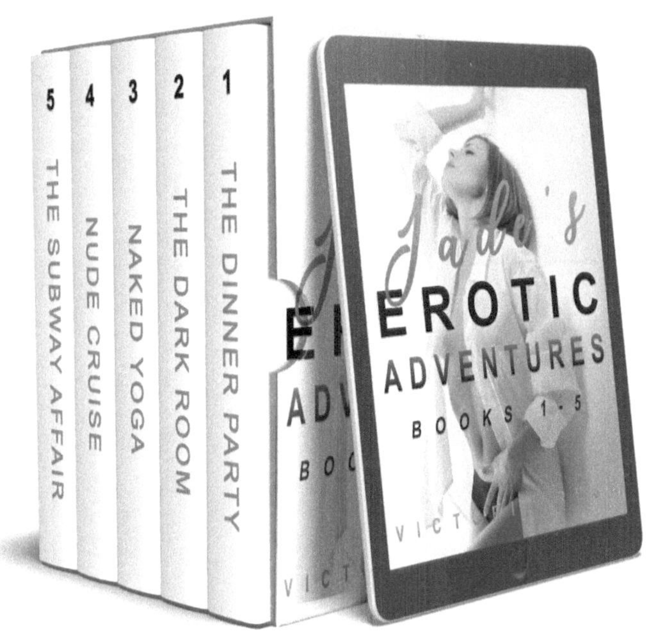

Books 1 -5 in the bestselling series - 60% off

For the uninhibited...

1

———————

"Every time I see you, I want to tell one of those bad gynecologist jokes," I said to my sex therapist friend Hannah at our weekly luncheon.

Hannah rolled her eyes as she took another bite of her salad. Her practice seemed to be the never-ending butt of jokes among our friends, but she'd learned to take the digs with good humor.

"Well you know I'm a far cry from a gynecologist, but I could use a little laugh today, so if you really need to get it out of your system, lay it on me."

"Ok, so this old lady goes to see her dentist," I started. "When her appointment is called, she sits in the chair, lowers her underpants, and raises her legs..."

"Uh huh," Hannah murmured, lifting a glass of soda water to her lips to signal her disinterest.

"So the dentist says," I continued, 'Excuse me, but I'm not a gynecologist.'"

I paused long enough for Hannah to begin swallowing her water. "'I know,' said the old lady. 'I want you to take my husband's teeth out.'"

Hannah lurched forward, spewing her soda water all over her salad as she raised her hand to her mouth, coughing loudly.

"Are you okay?" I said, glancing at the surrounding restaurant patrons alarmed by the sudden commotion at our table.

"Y–yeah," Hannah gagged. "The water just went down the wrong way. I wasn't expecting that punchline."

"Pretty good, right?" I smiled.

"Better than most, I'll grant you," she nodded. "But I don't know why you guys always make fun of my practice. *Someone* has to help all the sexually dysfunctional people out there."

"I know," I said, frowning sheepishly. "It's just hard to imagine what goes on in your office when people talk candidly about their sex lives."

"You'd be surprised," Hannah said, taking another swig of water to clear her throat. "In fact, I was thinking of inviting you to one of my sessions sometime."

I pinched my eyebrows and shook my head, surprised at her offer.

"As a *patient* or as an observer?"

"You don't need any help with your sex life," she said. "You're already miles ahead of me with all your wild escapades and adventures. I'd like to present you as more of a role model for what a healthy, sexually uninhibited person looks like."

"What would you have me *do* exactly? Don't you have to protect patient-doctor privilege? I thought you guys had to keep everything at arms-length, so to speak."

"I've been experimenting with some different strategies lately," Hannah smiled. "Let's just say I've been trying out some more *active* therapeutic techniques."

"No way!" I said, widening my eyes as I rested my cocktail on the table so as not to spill it. "Isn't that against the rules? I thought you had to maintain a certain degree of professional distance or risk losing your license."

"I still do. The only difference is now I encourage them to practice some of the prescribed self-empowerment techniques in my *office* instead of at home, so I can coach and guide them more actively. Besides, everybody signs a waiver before we take it to the next level."

"Holy shit!" I said, shaking my glass incredulously. "While you *watch* them touch themselves intimately?"

"Sometimes," Hannah nodded. "But most patients prefer to be concealed behind a protective screen when they first start the process."

"So you basically guide them through a facilitated *masturbation* session?"

"In a manner of speaking, yes. I find most patients need a little more active engagement to get them over the hump becoming comfortable enjoying sex with another person. You'd be surprised how many sexually dysfunctional women there are out there."

"So most of your patients are women?"

"Yes–I find them much more interesting to work with."

"Oh my God," I panted, beginning to feel my panties moisten under my tight jeans. "I'd love to be a fly on the wall in one of these sessions. How do you manage to stay focused when things start to heat up? Don't you get aroused while these women pleasure themselves?"

Hannah shifted uncomfortably in her chair, signaling for the waiter to bring her another cocktail.

"I do. At first, I just kind of squirmed in my chair and squeezed my legs together in frustration. But I've discovered a more animated way to keep myself stimulated while I watch my patients enjoying themselves."

My eyes flew open as the fluid in my cocktail glass began to tremble.

"You stick a *vibrator* down your pants?!" I said. "Isn't that kind of noisy? How do you hide that from your patients?"

"It's not just *any* vibrator," Hannah said with a crooked grin. "Our friend Cheryl from the local Babeland store introduced me to a new kind of toy. It's designed by a woman to mimic the touch and movement of real fingers and lips. It doesn't buzz so much as *hum* as it undulates both inside and on the outside of your vulva."

"Jesus!" I squealed, furrowing my brow in frustration. "Just when I thought I had the full collection of the latest toys. What does this thing look like?"

Hannah opened up her purse and passed me a large finger-shaped device attached to a hollow cone at the base.

"I just happen to carry one with me wherever I go," she said. "See for yourself."

I peered at the strange-looking object, stroking the soft silicone surface gently.

"It sure doesn't look like anything I've seen before. How does it work if it doesn't vibrate?"

"The long finger-shaped appendage goes inside you and bends in a series of come-hither motions against your G-spot. Give it a try by tapping the control button on the base one time."

I pressed the button and the finger began waving toward me like some kind of animatronic alien finger.

"*What the fuck*?" I said. "That's insane! It moves just like a real finger. And it hardly makes a sound."

"That the best part. You can use it anywhere. Even in a

crowded restaurant. You should give it a try. Pretend that you're reclining on a couch in my office."

I glanced around the table to make sure no one else had seen the strange device that I was fondling at the table.

"It's tempting," I said, peering into the orifice at the top of the cone. "But what's with this little hole near the bottom of the device? What goes on there?"

"See for yourself," Hannah smiled. "Tap the button a second time. You might be in for a bit of a surprise."

I tapped the button again and a long, tongue-shaped object pushed up out of the hole and began undulating like a hypnotic snake against my palm.

My eyes grew wide as saucers as Hannah nodded at me with a huge smirk.

"Like I said," she grinned. "It's not a vibrator so much as a *replicator*. Doesn't it remind you of a real finger and tongue?"

"In a weird, perverted, *ET* kind of way–yeah."

Hannah lowered her gaze and nodded toward my midsection.

"You've got to feel it down there to really appreciate it. Go ahead–give it a try. No one needs to know besides us girls."

"Seriously?" I said. "Right here?!"

"Why not? There's a long skirt surrounding the table. You can loosen your pants and insert it inside you without anyone knowing. Let me have a little bit of fun watching you pleasure yourself for a change. We haven't been together that way in quite a while."

"I have to admit," I huffed. "I *am* insanely horny right now. I'm dying to try this thing out. But what are you going to do while I amuse myself?"

"I'm going to eat my salad like we're having a normal

luncheon. This is all about *you* girl, don't worry about me. Knock yourself out."

"I can't believe I'm thinking about doing this," I said, watching the tongue slither back into its hole as I turned the toy off temporarily.

"It should be pretty easy to insert it if you're already properly worked up," Hannah said, lifting her glass to her lips.

I glanced to both sides of our table to make sure nobody else was watching, then reached under the tablecloth and unzipped my jeans, pulling them down to the floor. I could feel my juices already pooling on the wooden chair between my legs as I lowered the device under the table.

"Just be sure to position it so the hole is over your clit," Hannah whispered.

"I'm all over that," I nodded, slowly inserting the bulbous tip into my opening.

It slipped inside my slit smoothly, and I gasped as I pushed it all the way up inside me.

"It's not like just *any* old finger, is it?" Hannah grinned.

"No," I panted. "It's longer and fatter than most."

"It's designed with the ideal shape and form to stimulate your G-spot. If you've got it pressed all the way inside, turn it on to see what it feels like when it's animated."

I glanced around me nervously, watching the other restaurant patrons lost in conversation with their partners.

"Are you sure I'm going to be able to control myself in full view of all these customers? What if I break out into a Meg Ryan in front of all these people?"

"That'll be up to you to keep things under control as much as you can. But if not, what's the worst that can happen? Just like in the movie, everybody will want to know what you ordered that made you so happy."

"Very funny," I said, fumbling to find the control button on the base of the unit resting over my mound.

I pressed the button and began squirming in my chair as the long pointed finger began caressing me like no lover I ever had.

"Uhnn," I groaned, feeling the unusual stimulation inside my pussy.

"Not too bad, is it?" Hannah smiled. "Imagine all that going on while you're watching one of my patients pleasuring themselves."

"Is that really *possible*?" I said, getting even more turned on at the thought of watching one of her clients playing with herself in Hannah's private office.

"I've been thinking about it for a while," Hannah nodded. "It's the logical next step in the process of learning to become fully functional in a paired relationship. I've already had a few of my patients suggest they'd like me to guide them through their first encounter with another partner."

"You know how I like to *watch*," I groaned, as my eyes began to glaze over from the delicate sensation of the long finger rubbing up against my G-spot.

Hannah crossed her legs under the table and began to bob up and down as she flexed her buttocks and thighs together watching me get off.

"I do," she said, lifting her cocktail glass off the table and sliding her tongue around the rim suggestively. "Try the tongue action now."

"You're such a tease," I hissed, reaching under the table-cloth and tapping the control button one more time.

When I felt the flexible appendage push out of the hole and begin rolling over my hard clit, I bent over my place setting, grasping the handles of my chair tightly.

"That's it, babe," Hannah purred. "Feel the rhythm. Close your eyes and imagine it's your fantasy partner licking your pussy. Surrender to the feeling..."

"Is this how you do it with your clients?" I panted. "Talking to them all sexy while they play with themselves?"

"Sometimes," Hannah smiled. "Or sometimes I just let them do most of the vocalization while they tell me what they're doing behind the screen."

I spread my knees further apart imagining myself in one of her sessions.

"Do they ever get to the point where they're comfortable letting you watch them?"

"That's the ultimate goal. I've had a number of clients reach that level already. But I'd like to try taking it one step further. That's where you come in–"

"Tell me, Han," I moaned, beginning to lose myself in the fantasy. "Tell me what you want me to do with your sexy patients."

"We'll start out slowly at first," she instructed. "We'll just have you listen to them moan and purr as they begin the process of self-discovery behind the safety of their protective screen. But you'll have to be quiet at first to not distract their self-focus."

"At *this* point," I said, beginning to feel the pleasure spreading over my entire body. "That might be enough. With this amazing device doing its thing, I could probably get off listening to the sound of running water."

"That's the intent," Hannah laughed. "At least for my clients. But in order for them to become truly uninhibited and be able to function competently, the next step would be for the two of you to emerge from your hiding places and become comfortable watching each other in a face-to-face setting."

"*Fuck, yes,*" I panted. "If I can help another soul learn to enjoy the full pleasures of lesbian sex, count me in!"

"I know *you* won't have any trouble participating in this next phase of the process," Hannah smiled. "Just try to keep some of your more extreme methods in check for a while so you don't scare away my customers."

"I promise to keep my big dildos at home if you insist," I smirked.

"Once we get them feeling comfortable touching themselves and achieving climax in this voyeur scenario, the last step will be for the two of you to join together on the same couch and explore each other with more direct contact."

"Can I break out some of my favorite moves then?"

"If you find your partner is responding appropriately. Just be careful to always be gentle and focused on her needs. If you get to the point where she feels comfortable getting more inventive, by all means–"

"Oh, I've got the *means* alright," I moaned, imaging myself straddling one of her patients with her legs splayed wide apart as we ground our pussies together and I watched her come all over me. "How soon can we set this up?"

"I've got a certain patient in mind. She's young and never been with another woman before. She's had some unfulfilling experiences with men and confided that she's always fantasized about being with a woman. We'll just have to ease her into it carefully. Are you up for the opportunity, assuming she's game?"

"You know I am," I grunted, pressing harder down against the artificial tongue. "But first, tell me more about this girl..."

"She's nineteen, a sophomore in college, with a cheerleader's body–"

"She's athletic then?"

"Oh yes," Hannah smiled. "Tight ass, firm tits, and legs that could wrap all the way around you while you tribbed her virgin pussy–"

"Oh God, Han," I moaned. "I can't take it any longer. Sign me up–I want to taste her sweet pussy in my mouth..."

"Yes, Jade," Hannah purred. "Let it go, hun. Surrender to the feeling–"

As I imagined the co-ed writhing in ecstasy sitting on my face, the pleasure generated by the lifelike sex toy suddenly peaked, and I bit my lip as I began convulsing in my chair. I'd never fought so hard to remain quiet during a powerful orgasm in my entire life. There was something about the experience of cumming surrounded by scores of oblivious restaurant patrons that made the experience all the more erotic. While I twisted and squirmed in my chair, Hannah smiled as she raised her glass in toast to me.

"Congratulations, Jade," she said. "You've just passed the first test with flying colors."

2

With every passing day after our luncheon, I grew increasingly excited about the idea of participating in one of Hannah's guided therapy sessions. When she finally called me back, I almost dropped my phone fumbling to answer it.

"Han?" I answered the phone expectantly.

"Are you sure you're up for this?" Hannah asked.

"Are you kidding me?" I said. "It's all I've been thinking about since I last saw you."

"I've got another session scheduled with my target client for this Thursday at eleven a.m. Are you available?"

"With the young co-ed?"

"Yes."

"Absolutely!" I gushed.

"Ok," Hannah said. "We're going to have to set this up carefully. I don't want to put too much pressure on either one of you during this initial encounter. I think it's better if she doesn't even know you're there at first. I'll talk to her while she begins to explore her body behind the safety of the protective screen, then broach the subject of introducing a potential partner at the next session."

"Okay," I said. "But where will you hide me?"

"As strange as it may sound, I think the only safe place to be sure you're not discovered is in my closet. You can open the door a crack and listen if you promise to be absolutely quiet the entire time. That way, I can protect her identity in the event she doesn't wish to escalate things to the next level."

I shook my head at the idea of spying on her like a peeping Tom, but the dampness in my panties betrayed my true feelings.

"I'll feel like a bit of a lech hiding in the closet, but if that's what it'll take to make sure she's comfortable, I can work with that."

"Okay then," Hannah said. "Meet me at my office at 10:45 and I'll get you situated. And remember–not even a peep."

"I promise to be on my best behavior," I smiled. "If I can stay silent surrounded by a hundred restaurant customers, I think I can handle one uptight schoolgirl."

"And don't bring any toys either. I don't want to take the chance she'll hear anything other than my soothing voice."

"Not even your special vibrator that doesn't make any noise?"

"I'm not sure I can trust you with that thing. Besides, it's already going to be put to good use while you're in the closet."

"No fair!" I protested. "*You'll* be the one having all the fun!"

"I'm sure you can find other ways to amuse yourself," Hannah said. "You'll have plenty of chances to get more actively engaged during the next session. Just don't trip over anything in there when things start to heat up."

As soon as Hannah hung up, I rushed into my bedroom and positioned my dressing room mirror in front of my clothes closet. Then I opened the door a crack and imagined it was the schoolgirl I was watching while I jilled myself to a quick orgasm.

This should be interesting, I thought, quivering in the darkness. *I just hope her patient will find it as erotic as I do, knowing someone else is on the other side of the curtain.*

On the day of the scheduled session, I arrived fifteen minutes early as requested, while Hannah reiterated the ground rules and gave me final instructions. She made me promise that I wouldn't open the door until her client was safely behind the protective screen. She knew she was already pushing the boundary of professional ethics, and she wanted to make sure that her patient's identity would be protected until the girl felt comfortable introducing another person into the mix.

When I got into the closet, I pushed the coats to one side to produce an open space for me, then I peered through the louvers as I heard a soft tap on Hannah's office door. The slats were angled downward, so I could only see the floor a few feet ahead of me, but that was enough to get my heart racing in excitement already.

"Good morning, Haley," I heard Hannah say as two shadows crossed the floor in front of me. "Can I get you a coffee or tea? It's a bit chilly out there today, and you probably need to warm up."

"I'm fine, thank you," a young woman's voice spoke softly. "I'm pretty nervous about today's session and I don't think I should be holding any hot beverages in my trembling hands."

"There's no need to worry," Hannah assured the girl. "We're going to take things slowly, at your own pace. May I take your coat?"

"Yes, thank you," the girl said.

I heard the rustling of clothes then the sound of footfalls moving toward the closet. The door on the opposite side of the closet opened and Hannah reached in to fetch an open hanger, then she hung the girl's coat over the crossbar. I could smell her perfume on the garment, and my pussy twitched when I realized how close she was to me on the other side of the door. But neither Hannah nor I so much as made eye contact, to protect the secrecy of our little ruse.

"Have a seat, please," Hannah said, and I heard the sound of the girl reclining on the office divan.

"If you remember from our last session," Hannah continued, "we talked about trying something a little different today. You shared your discomfort about touching yourself intimately based on your prior family history, and that you thought it might be helpful to have me coach you through a private session. Are you still feeling comfortable taking it to this next level?"

"I think so," Haley said. "But you mentioned the possibility of my having a bit more privacy. I'm not sure I'm ready to have you watch me just yet."

"Of course," Hannah said. "It'll be easier for you to concentrate on exploring your body and focus on what you're feeling without any outside distractions. I can move the linen screen between the two of us to protect your privacy, but I'd also like to place this long dressing mirror in front of your couch so you can watch yourself and begin to get more comfortable with your body. Will that work for you?"

"I suppose so," Haley said, hesitating. "Do you have any expectations for today's session? I mean, in terms of achieving climax or anything like that?"

"None whatsoever," Hannah said. "This is all about you becoming comfortable in your own skin and beginning the process of self-exploration. The only desire I have is that you learn to relax and accept the beauty of your own body. This is a journey, not a destination. You need to learn how to love *yourself* before you can begin to think about loving someone else."

Oh, she's good, I thought. If only every girl could have this kind of advice when they're first experiencing the strange feelings of puberty and early adulthood. Far too many parents make their kids think sex is dirty and that enjoying any kind of carnal pleasure before marriage is sinful. For a moment, I reflected back on my own awkward attempts at sex with my first husband, realizing how much time and pleasure I'd forsaken until I learned to explore my sexuality on my own and with other like-minded women.

I listened to the sound of furniture moving across the floor as Hannah positioned the mirror in front of Haley's settee then placed the curtain between their two chairs.

"Does that make you feel more comfortable?" Hannah asked the girl.

"Yes, thank you," Haley said.

"Good. Now first, I just want you to look at yourself fully clothed in the mirror. Look at your pretty face and the curves of your figure and recognize that you're a beautiful woman who was designed to enjoy the natural pleasures of your body. And that this is also part of the natural process of pairing with a partner and enjoying the shared union that is part of the human experience."

"Okay..." Haley said with a hesitating lilt.

As I listened to her soft voice, my mind raced imagining what she looked like lying on the divan, watching herself in the mirror.

"But first you need to get fully comfortable in your own skin," Hannah said. "And begin to experience the pleasures that you've been naturally endowed with as a healthy young woman. Unfortunately, our society has learned to cover up our bodies as if they're a shameful thing we should hide. I want you to see your body as a beautiful thing and recognize the pleasures it can deliver to you, both when you're alone and with a partner."

Damn straight, I thought, feeling the blood rushing to my pussy as I reflected back on my own first tentative explorations of my young body that led to my first climax.

"Now I want you to take off your blouse and your bra,'"Hannah continued. "And lie back against the chair as you examine your body and begin to explore some of your erogenous areas."

I heard the sound of soft rustling behind the screen, followed by awkward silence.

"Can you see your naked torso in the mirror in front of you?" Hannah asked.

"Yes..." Haley said softly.

"Look at your breasts and examine their shape. Did you know that every woman has her own unique shape? Some have large breasts, some have small breasts, some have pointy breasts, and some have floppy breasts. It's all part of the female expression and what makes you unique."

More awkward silence.

"Do you like the shape of your breasts, Haley?" Hannah said.

"I suppose so…"

"I want you to cup them in your hands and feel how soft and pleasant they feel to be held and coddled. A woman's breasts are a beautiful thing, and they serve many purposes. Besides feeding a newborn child, their shape is meant to attract other partners whose bodies you can likewise enjoy and appreciate. And of course, your breasts can be a source of intense internal pleasure for yourself. Did you know that some women can climax just from the feeling of their babies suckling on their teats?"

"I had no idea," Haley said.

While Hannah talked the girl through the process of self-examination, I mimicked her movements and gestures, trying to imagine how she felt and how her body was responding. I unbuttoned my blouse and opened my bra, feeling an electric charge race through my body as I felt the fullness of my breasts in my hands.

"Now I want you to pinch your nipples gently between your thumbs and forefingers as you cup your breasts and roll them between your fingers, telling me what you feel."

"It tingles a little bit," Haley confessed.

"In a good way?"

"Yes–I think so."

"Do you notice any changes to the size and shape of your nipples?"

"Yes," Haley said. "They're growing larger and firmer."

"That's another one of the amazing reactions our bodies experience when our erogenous zones are properly stimulated. Do you like the feeling when you touch your breasts in this way, Haley?"

"Yes," she panted softly.

The girl's visceral reaction to touching herself sent a chill down my spine as I felt myself getting wetter and wetter by the moment.

"Look at your body in the mirror as you touch yourself. Do you see your chest flushing and your breasts subtly changing shape?"

"Yes."

"That's from your blood rushing to the area to provide more oxygen and nutrients to feed the increased stimulation. Isn't it wonderful how our bodies naturally respond when we stimulate it in a pleasant way?"

"Mmm," Haley purred.

"Now I want you to bend your head down and lift one of your breasts toward your mouth. You've been blessed with larger breasts than most, and if you can suck and lick your nipples, I want you to tell me how it feels."

Soon after, I heard the sound of liquid sloshing and the smacking of lips. I knew that Haley was sucking her plump nipples, and the thought of it sent rivers of fluid running down the inside of my legs. I was glad that I'd chosen to wear a dress instead of jeans so I'd have freer access to my pussy in the tight confines of Hannah's closet.

"How does that feel?" Hannah asked.

"Heavenly," Haley sighed. "I've never really explored my body in this way before."

"You'll be amazed at all the ways you and your partner can create exciting sensations like these using different techniques and body parts to explore the different areas of your body. Look up at your nipples in the mirror every now and then, but don't let me stop you from continuing your exploration."

I could hear the sloshing and smacking sounds increasing in frequency and pitch, along with Haley's moans and sighs. I had to bite my lip to keep from moaning myself, as I imagined what she must have been feeling at this moment.

"What do you see and feel?" Hannah asked.

"The dark ring around my nipples is getting smaller and my nipples are getting harder the more I lick and suck them."

"Mmm, that's good," Hannah said.

I could tell Hannah was getting just as turned on as I was from the exchange, and I wondered if she'd turned on her vibrator yet.

"Mix up the way you stimulate your nipples," she said. "Try circling your tongue around the perimeter and flicking it over the ends of your nipples every now and then. Most of the pleasure in exploring our bodies is discovered from the many different ways we can stimulate ourselves and others. Squeeze your breasts with your hands, pinch your nipples, suck and play with them as you lose yourself in the moment."

"It feels good," Haley panted. "I think I'm ready to try some of those other new techniques you mentioned now."

I smiled when I realized Haley was losing herself in the process and beginning to surrender to the pleasurable feelings flooding her body.

"Let's get comfortable seeing your *entire* body in the nude then," Hannah continued. "I want you to take off the rest of your clothes and throw them to the side. There are so many other ways to give yourself pleasure."

I heard some more rustling of clothes, this time more urgent-sounding, and the telltale sound of clothes dropping to the floor. It was obvious to me that Haley was getting more and more worked up and that she no longer cared if her clothes got a little wrinkled or dirty.

After the rustling sound stopped, Hannah paused for a moment to let the silence in the room escalate the sexual tension. Her professional technique was working for more than just her client, as I froze with my hand still as a statue against my dripping pussy while I imagined the pretty schoolgirl looking at her naked body on the chaise lounge chair.

"Are you fully naked now, Haley?" Hannah asked.

"Yes," the girl said.

"Examine the curve of your profile for a moment. See the way your waist tapers and the swelling of your hips above your long, shapely legs. Do you think you're beautiful, Haley?"

"Yes," she said. "I feel good all over."

"Good," Hannah said. "Now I want you to spread your legs and knees apart a little bit so you can examine your private area. Can you see your skin glistening on your vulva and on the inside of your thighs?"

"Yes," Haley panted.

"That means your body is enjoying the stimulation you've provided so far and that you're feeling aroused viewing your own body. Can you see the slit between your legs?"

"Yes–"

"I want you to run your hands gently down the front of your torso, feeling the softness of the skin on your abdomen..."

"My tummy is trembling," Haley said.

"That's a natural reaction to the excitement you feel as you caress yourself and move closer to your magical place."

"Magical place?"

"You'll see what I mean soon enough. Can you see the natural hairs covering your private area?"

"Yes," Haley said.

Both Hannah and I guessed that a girl this young and innocent wouldn't have learned yet to trim her pubic hair in the manner of the modern custom.

"I want you to run your fingers through your bush and tell me what you feel."

For a moment I envied the virgin schoolgirl with her natural muff. It had been a long time since I'd felt the wonderful feeling of my pubic hairs being caressed and stroked in this way. By way of consolation, I raised my slippery fingers up from my crotch and spread my juices over my bare mound.

"It feels kind of ticklish," Haley said from behind the screen. "But in a good way. I feel all warm and tingly inside."

"That's your body's way of saying it's enjoying the sensation of being touched this way. Now the blood is rushing to an entirely different area of your body. Can you feel yourself becoming wetter and wetter around your opening?"

"Yes," Haley said. "It's a good thing you put a blanket down over your chair. Otherwise, I'd be making a mess of your pretty office."

"That's perfect," Hannah said. "I'd like nothing more than for you to make a mess of my office. That just means that you're enjoying the experience and that your body is reacting the way it was meant to."

"I can feel things beginning to heat up down there," Haley grunted. "And there's other changes too–"

"Spread your legs further apart now and tell me what changes you see. And what you *feel*."

"I can see my lips are getting wetter and darker. And my little bean is getting plumper and harder. I feel like I'm tingling all over now..."

"Move your hands between your thighs and feel the slippery wetness as you caress the sides of your labia. How does that feel?"

"It feels *good*," Haley panted. "It's so warm and wet. I'm feeling some other sensations now..."

"Isn't it wonderful how good you can make yourself feel just by gently exploring your body and appreciating your natural beauty?"

"Yes, Dr. Marshall."

"Please, call me Hannah. At this point, we don't need to stay so informal, plus it will make it easier for you to vocalize what you're feeling. Now, I want you to explore a very special place on your body. Trace your fingers up along the edges of your labia until they meet at the top, then touch your little nub and tell me what you feel."

"*Huh!*" Haley gasped. "Oh, that feels–different. It's a much more intense type of tingling now."

By now I was rubbing my button furiously as I imagined Haley playing with her clit for the first time. As I peered through the slats trying desperately to catch any sight of her shadow or movement on the reflective floor, I could hear the soft sound of my own juices as I became more and more excited by the sensory deprivation of being locked in the closet.

"Yes," Hannah said, encouraging Haley on. "We women are lucky to be endowed with the most sensitive organ on the human body. Our clitorises are bestowed with more than eight thousand nerve endings–more per square inch than even on the end of a man's penis. Rub your fingers softly over your jewel and close your eyes as you savor the feeling."

"Oh God," Haley moaned. "That feels so good. I had no idea I could make myself feel this way."

"We're just getting started exploring all the possibilities,"

Hannah said, her own voice starting to become ragged. "Run your fingers over your clit, trying different movements. Sometimes it's nice to pinch it gently between your fingers, and sometimes it feels good to rub your fingers in circles over your button. Can you see anything *else* changing in your vulva as you rub yourself this way?"

"Yes," Haley groaned. "My lips are getting puffier, and they're beginning to separate a bit."

"*Fuck me,*" I groaned under my breath, wishing I could be looking into the same mirror that Haley was viewing at this precise moment. *How I'd love to fuck her sweet little pussy right now.*

"That's perfectly normal and healthy," Hannah purred. "That's just your body's way of saying that it's ready to accept another partner into the equation. Do you think you'd like to try that someday soon?"

"Maybe," Haley said. "But right now I'm having too much fun all by myself. I'm beginning to feel some different feelings now. The tingling is getting much more intense. It almost feels like I have to pee or something..."

"That means you're getting closer to reaching the apex of your pleasure," Hannah said, shifting in her chair. "Close your eyes now and focus on your body as you surrender to the pleasure. Don't worry if things start to get pretty intense. Just lose yourself in the process..."

"Yes, doc–I mean Hannah," Haley squeaked. "I feel it now. It feels like a wave is falling over me. A big, beautiful wall of pleasure engulfing me..."

"Yes, Haley," Hannah mewed. "Let it consume you. Surrender to the passion inside your body."

"Oh God! Oh God!" Haley whimpered. "It feels so good. Something is happening. I feel it coming over me–. Uhnnn! Uhnnn! Uhnnn!"

As I listened to Haley having her first powerful orgasm, I lost all control and began squirting over the floor of Hannah's closet as my pussy clamped together in multiple contractions while I leaned against the wall to steady myself. I'd never heard anything so erotic in my entire life, and my whole body was trembling at the thought of meeting her face-to-face at our next session.

When Haley finally stopped moaning and silence filled the room, I could hear Hannah shifting again in her chair. I wondered if she'd been unable to control herself and had had a powerful orgasm of her own listening to Haley. With that lifelike sex toy embedded in her pussy, I couldn't imagine how she'd able to hold back.

"How does it feel to experience the natural pleasures of being a woman, Haley?" she said.

"Oh my God," Haley panted. "I had no idea I had this inside of me. I want more–"

"There's so much more for you to experience, young lady. I encourage you to experiment with more self-exploration before our next session. Of course, the ultimate pleasure of being a woman happens when you get to *share* this pleasure with another partner. Do you think you might be ready to try this at our next meeting?"

"Um–maybe. But how will that work? I don't think I'm quite ready to jump right into an intimate relationship with a complete stranger."

"With your permission," Hannah said, "I'd like to invite another patient to the session who's expressed similar feelings about being with another woman. We can start slowly at first with the two of you just watching and talking to one another before we consider taking it to the next stage. You should always feel completely comfortable with your partner before agreeing to share this kind of intimacy."

"That does sound interesting," Haley said. "Would we be separated by protective screens again?"

"Only if you both want it that way. But something tells me you're ready to discover for yourself how much higher it can elevate the experience watching another woman pleasuring herself with you at the same time."

"Yes," Haley said. "I think I might like that."

"Let me know before your next session if you'd like to meet this new girl. Because she's definitely ready to meet you."

No shit, I muttered under my breath as my pussy continued spasming over my fingers firmly embedded inside my hole.

I had no idea know how I'd be able to keep it together for a whole week before I met this girl again. I smiled as my juices streamed down the insides of my thighs.

I'll just have to practice as much as I can in the meantime to get ready.

3

____

The intervening week before Haley's next scheduled session felt like the longest week of my life. I couldn't stop thinking about what she looked like and how she'd react to watching me respond to Hannah's instruction the way she had. I spent long hours lying on my couch with my dressing mirror propped up in front of me, fantasizing that it was Haley watching me instead of myself.

I must have cum a hundred times contorting myself into different positions trying to make myself look as sexy and alluring as possible. I didn't want to take any chance that she wouldn't respond positively to me in this shared therapy session. Beyond my desire for her to enjoy the experience to the fullest extent possible, I didn't want anything getting in the way of her moving on to the final step in her journey of sexual awakening. Every time I thought about actually touching her, my pussy throbbed and I had to tear my clothes off once again to quell the yearning desire within me.

When the appointment day finally arrived, I spent most

of the morning trying on different outfits I thought might strike the right balance between sexually enticing and emotionally guarded. After all, Hannah was presenting me as another repressed patient who'd reached out for help overcoming her fear of intimacy with other women. I finally decided on a pleated mid-length skirt with inch-high pumps and a creamy silk blouse that hugged my breasts just enough to highlight the fullness of my bosom.

Hannah had asked me to arrive at her office five minutes after the hour so she could prep Haley first and confirm that she still wished to proceed as intended. The plan was for her to send me a quick text with either a smiling or frowning emoji to signal her readiness. When I still hadn't heard anything by 11:15, I shifted uncomfortably in her waiting room, wondering if Haley had gotten cold feet.

I couldn't blame her if she had. This whole idea was highly irregular and must have been kind of frightening for her. It was a far cry from meeting someone the natural way, getting to know them over a period of time before deciding to initiate intimate relations. But if she was too afraid to approach another woman the traditional way, I had every intention of making this experience as comfortable and uplifting as possible.

When my phone pinged and I saw the smiley-face symbol in my message thread, I stood up and nervously smoothed out the wrinkles in my blouse. I chuckled at the realization that I was just as anxious as the young schoolgirl at the prospect of our chaperoned playdate. Hannah stuck her head out her office door motioning me inside, and I straightened myself out and walked confidently into her office.

The girl was standing a few feet to Hannah's side, smiling nervously at me when our eyes met. I was surprised how young she looked in her skinny jeans, tight t-shirt, and Keds sneakers. She had long blonde hair, big bright eyes, and the plump skin of an adolescent who hadn't lost any of her youthful collagen. I must have looked ancient almost fifteen years older than her, as I pulled my shoulders back trying to lift my chest and press my breasts against my tight blouse.

Hannah turned toward the girl, arcing her arm toward me.

"Haley," she said. "This is Jade. In spite of your difference in age, I think you'll find you actually have a lot in common. I've brought the two of you together today to share some of your mutual experiences and learn to become more comfortable expressing your intimacy in the presence of another woman."

Hannah peered at the two of us and smiled.

"Would you like a drink before we get started?"

"Have you got some *tequila* behind your bar?" I joked.

"That might not be such a bad idea to help you both loosen up," Hannah chuckled. "But unfortunately, all I have to offer is coffee or tea."

"I'll have a coffee with a bit of cream and sugar then," I said.

"Tea is fine," Haley nodded.

"Cream and sugar also?" Hannah asked.

"Yes, thank you."

As Hannah turned to prepare our drinks, I moved closer toward Haley and extended my hand. She looked even prettier up close, with thick natural eyebrows and long dark lashes.

"Pleased to meet you, Haley," I said. "Hannah's told me so much about you. You're even more beautiful than she described."

Haley reached out and clasped my hand softly, and I could feel the nervous dampness in her palm as we touched for the first time.

"Thank you," she said. "You're very pretty also."

Her eyes blinked as she stole a glance down my body, peering at the cleavage formed by my push-up bra peeking out of my loosely unbuttoned blouse. My breasts were at least full size larger than hers, and I stood three or four inches taller in my elevated pumps.

"You remind me a little of Marilyn Monroe in that white blouse and skirt," she said.

"That's very kind," I smiled. "I could never hold a candle to her, though I feel a certain affinity given my own little seven-year-itch. It took me at least that long to break free of the oppressive bonds of my first marriage."

"Have you married again?"

"No–I guess I'm still discovering myself. I've kind of been looking for a change of pace lately. I never felt fully satisfied in my relationships with men."

"I've never felt comfortable approaching *either* gender, actually. My parents were pretty strict about the whole dating thing when I was growing up–"

Hannah returned from her kitchen and handed each of us a steaming mug.

"I see you two are beginning to get more comfortable," she said. "I'm glad to see you hitting it off so quickly. Would you like to get more comfortable?"

Haley and I turned to see two long chaise lounge chairs facing one another about ten feet apart, angled slightly toward Hannah's armchair positioned at the apex of the triangle. I smiled when I realized she'd done this intentionally to facilitate her own enhanced viewing of the two of us once we got loosened up.

We walked toward the settees and I paused, motioning for Haley to take the one on the left side. Both chairs were covered in a long throw blanket, and I kicked off my shoes before sitting back against the curved backrest, crossing my ankles on the end nearest Haley. It felt awkward holding my coffee in this semi-reclined position, and when I leaned over to rest it on the floor beside me, Haley did the same.

"How are you both feeling today?" Hannah said as she sat in her chair in front of us, crossing her legs sexily with her pointed pumps bouncing gently in our direction.

I had little doubt she was wearing her special sex toy under her prim business suit, and I envied her for a moment, knowing she'd have a leg up on the two of us for the rest of the session.

"Good," Haley said, with a gentle lilt.

"Better *now*," I said, smiling toward Haley.

"You've both expressed interest in exploring a same-sex relationship, but also about your reservations initiating the process given your previous experiences."

I nodded, realizing there was more than a hint of truth in her statement, even though I'd long since resolved my reticence about being with other women.

"The purpose of this session is to give you both an opportunity to become more comfortable in the presence of another woman, and to the extent you feel ready, to begin to explore the boundaries of your sexuality in the safe confines of my office. Is this still something you both feel comfortable proceeding with?"

I looked at Haley and she peered back at me, as we both nodded gently.

"Okay," Hannah said. "At first, I'd just like the two of you to gaze into each other's eyes for a moment and pause as you take a moment to acknowledge each other as willing partners and make a silent connection..."

I smiled at Haley and saw a soft flush spread over her cheeks as her pupils began to widen while she peered back at me. Even though neither of us said a thing, the longer I looked at her the more excited I got as my chest began rising and falling from my elevated respiration rate.

"Now, I want each of you to take a minute to look over each other's bodies without making any judgements or feeling self-conscious that you're checking each other out. Take a moment to appreciate the different shapes of your respective figures, and listen to how your body is reacting as you soak each other up."

I was happy to be given free license to leer at Haley's youthful figure, and as my eyes drifted down her body, I could feel my panties begin to moisten in excitement seeing the girl of my dreams reclining directly in front of me. Her breasts looked like they were painted on her body, sitting high and firm under her tight t-shirt. She had a narrow waist and slim but shapely hips, tapering to slender hourglass-shaped legs, looking all the more toned resting gently on the firm surface of her settee.

She in turn ran her gaze all over my body, pausing to stare at my full breasts pushing up against the flimsy silk fabric of my blouse. For a moment, I wished I'd decided to go braless, so she could see how she was turning me on as my nipples pressed against the soft fabric of my lace bra. After a few seconds of lingering, her eyes traced a line further down my body, pausing at the bottom of my skirt's hemline, as if hoping to catch a glimpse into the shadow between my closed legs. When her gaze reached the bottom of my feet, I wiggled my toes playfully, and she did the same with her cute sneakers. Even though we hadn't said a thing to each other for several minutes, I felt like we were already beginning to bond over our strange circumstances.

"Take a moment to revel in the beauty and diversity of the female form," Hannah whispered. "Recognize that everyone is built differently, and that these differences contribute to making each of us all the more interesting and alluring. Can you see the natural beauty within each of your own bodies and in those of your partner?"

"Yes," Haley nodded, tracing her gaze once again up to my pointed breasts.

"Absolutely," I enthused.

"Let's take this to the next level then," Hannah said. "If you feel comfortable, I'd like each of you to remove your tops and lie back in your chair while you admire one another in your undergarments."

As I slowly began unbuttoning my blouse, Haley leaned forward, pulling her t-shirt over her shoulders. When she lifted it over her head, her blonde locks fell down over the front of her cream-colored sports bra. I was a little disappointed to see her covered up so tightly, but her bra only seemed to accentuate the firmness of her perky tits.

When I unfastened the last button on my blouse, I pulled my arms out one side at a time then leaned back against the soft backrest. It felt electrifying to rest there in my lacy bra as Haley ran her eyes lustily over my exposed chest and abdomen. My brassiere was low-cut enough that she could see the tops of my dark areolas, and they puckered slightly as my hard nipples began to lift the fabric away from my skin.

"Now look at each other's bodies more closely," Hannah intoned. "Examine the shape of each other's breasts, the curvature of your waists, and the smoothness of your stomachs. What do you see that appeals to your feminine senses?"

"I like the fullness of Jade's breasts," Haley purred. "And the way the top edge of her bra angles sexily down toward her cleavage."

"Yes," Hannah said, stretching the S out the end of the word. "Being a sensual woman means we can dress up in different ways to tease and excite our partners as a precursor to more intimate relations. What do you see in Haley's body that you find most attractive, Jade?"

I paused for a moment, examining her tight belly and the subtle striations in her stomach.

"I like the line running down the middle of her abdomen from the bottom of her bra to her belly button. I wish I could be that lean and sexy once again."

"That's the beauty we share as women of different generations. Some women are more lean and chiseled, while others are more full-bodied and curvy. It's all part of the magnificent palette of the human form and what makes it so interesting for each of us to experience. Are you beginning to imagine what lies further underneath?"

"Yes..." Haley said, her cheeks flushing a crimson red.

"Oh, very definitely yes," I sighed, wishing I could jump out of my seat and tear Haley's sports bra off with my own hands.

"If you're ready then, you may remove your brassieres and begin to get more comfortable being naked in the presence of one another."

Haley hesitated for a moment, looking at me to make the first move. Fortunately, the bra I'd chosen to wear had the closure at the front, and as I pressed my fingers together unhinging the clasp and spreading the cups apart to reveal my naked breasts, I heard Haley gasp a few feet away. Her reaction only excited me more as I peered down at my tits, seeing that my nipples had already hardened and extended to their full extent. I pulled my bra off my back and threw it on the floor, and my whole body started buzzing as Haley stared at my torso with wide eyes.

Within a few seconds, she felt emboldened enough to remove her own sports bra as she pinched her thumbs under the lower band and pulled it over her head in one swift movement. Her breasts jiggled softly on her chest and I marveled at how perfectly round and symmetrical they were. They looked bigger than I imagined when I saw her fully clothed, and I began to salivate as I leered at her creamy skin and her light-colored areolas. They'd already begun to bunch up in excitement, protruding like two erasers on the end of a pencil.

Hannah paused just long moment to give each of us a chance to soak up each other's bodies. I could see Haley's eyes darting excitedly between my points as a light dew formed at the top of her chest between her breasts. This just accentuated the youthful look of her glistening skin, glowing like a sexy goddess. As my mouth watered at the thought of taking her moist nipples into my mouth, another part of me began to grow rapidly wetter.

"What are you feeling as you look each other's naked bodies?" Hannah said, interrupting our thoughts.

"I'm thinking how much I want to touch Haley right now," I confessed.

"There'll be plenty of time for that soon enough," Hannah said, admonishing me gently. "What are you feeling at this moment, Haley?"

"I'm just..." Haley panted, her moist lips parting slightly. "I'm just amazed at how gorgeous Jade's tits–I mean *breasts* are. She's looks like a supermodel to me."

"It's okay to use informal terms to describe each other's bodies," Hannah nodded. "It helps to desensitize the experience and lose yourself more readily in the feelings of arousal that you're experiencing. Are you beginning to recognize how each of you are responding to the sight of watching one another in this manner?"

"Yes," Haley said as she locked her eyes on my tingling teats.

"You have *no* idea," I smiled, peering at Haley's quivering tummy.

"I'm happy you're both responding so positively. That means you're attracted to one another and that you're becoming more comfortable with the idea of exploring a different kind of union. Are you ready to take it to the next level?"

"I think so..." Haley hesitated.

"*God* yes," I panted, feeling the wetness in my panties beginning to run down the crack of my ass.

"Why don't you both take off your lower garments now, but keep your panties on for the moment? Part of the attraction with foreplay is taking our time to build the desire and teasing our partners by withholding those things we most crave. Take a moment to look at your naked bodies, but not completely undressed yet."

I leaned forward and unclasped the latch at the back of my skirt, then lowered the zipper and pulled my skirt down the front of my legs, throwing it playfully on the floor. Haley locked eyes on me as she unfastened the front of her jeans, wiggling sexily on her divan while she pulled her pants down, then flipping off her sneakers and throwing everything on the floor beside her.

She was wearing plain white low-cut panties that stretched at least four inches below her navel. I could see the dark outline of her bush under the thin fabric, and my pussy twitched knowing I'd soon get to see her completely naked. She leaned back and fixed her gaze on my crotch while I teasingly separated my feet a few inches. I was wearing matching lace panties and the light color must have shown the giant wet spot that had formed in the fabric. But I couldn't yet see any sign of wetness in Haley's underwear, since she still had her legs closed in a protective posture.

"How does it feel to view another woman like this, nearly naked?" Hannah asked. "Are you noticing any new reactions in your body as you watch your partner disrobe?"

"Yes," Haley panted. "I'm beginning to feel that same tingling sensation I experienced at our last session. It feels like my whole body is on fire..."

"How about you, Jade?" Hannah said, smiling at me. "How do you feel sitting in front of Haley almost naked?"

"Very sexy," I said. "I'm feeling things I haven't felt in a long time."

"So it would appear," she said, glancing at the wet spot between my legs. "Now I want each of you to spread your legs a little further apart to witness the effect you're having on one another. Take a moment to recognize the reaction each of you are experiencing as you become more and more aroused looking at one another's bodies."

As I spread my legs further apart, Haley pulled her feet up a few inches, then angled her knees down onto the divan to reveal the white swath of fabric running between her legs. I could see the indentation of her slit in the tight cotton and the telltale darkness of a small wet spot in the middle of her panties. Seeing her reveal this little slice of her private anatomy raised my excitement level even higher as the wet spot in my own panties slowly spread all the way from one side to the other.

While Haley stared at the widening dark spot between my legs, I noticed her chest begin to rise and fall as she started breathing more heavily. It took every ounce of my willpower to stay seated in my settee and not sprint over to her side and take her for myself. Hannah was right about one thing. All this slow buildup was driving me more crazy with desire and just increasing my longing to touch her.

"Can you see how each of you are responding to one another the more you reveal of yourselves?" Hannah said. "Are you beginning to become more comfortable with the idea of watching another woman being intimate and moving closer to a more formal connection?"

"Yes," Haley sighed.

"*Fuck*, yes," I gushed.

"Let's remove our remaining entrapments then and revel in the naked glory of the female body. You may both remove your last vestiges of clothing if you feel comfortable. Take a moment to soak up one another's bodies and connect with your feelings. A healthy sexual relationship starts with feeling comfortable in both your and your partner's nakedness."

I raised my hips, practically tearing my panties off as I pulled them down my legs and tossing them on the floor. While I kept my legs slightly parted, Haley wriggled out of her little white panties and dropped them sexily on the floor beside her. This time, she parted her legs the same distance as mine as we both stared at each other's wet slits shining in the bright overhead lights of Hannah's office. Haley's light pubic patch formed a perfect triangle over her mound and I clenched the fabric on the divan beside me trying to keep my hands from straying any further.

"There now," Hannah purred. "That wasn't so bad, was it?"

"No," Haley said. "It was actually easier than I imagined."

"How about you, Jade? How do you feel seeing your partner fully naked in front of you?"

"I'd hardly call it *easy*," I groaned. "The hardest part is remaining still on my sofa. My hands want to wander all over the place right now."

"If that's what you feel like doing, don't let me stop you from enjoying the process. I encourage each of you to begin touching yourselves while you verbalize how you're feeling. Communication and openness are the first two essential ingredients in any healthy relationship."

As I watched Haley separate her legs further apart, I lifted my hand to my breast and squeezed it tightly while I lowered my other hand to my crotch and began to circle my button. Normally I'd take more time to tease myself, but at this point I was so horny I needed to get right down to business.

Watching me touch myself and begin to moan softly seemed to encourage Haley, as she moved her hand to the inside of her thighs and began to flutter her fingers over her button. While we both began to moan and roll our hips over our divans, Hannah began to bob her foot more forcefully over her knee and cleared her throat.

"Yes," she mewed. "It's a beautiful thing watching another woman pleasuring herself. Focus on one another as you listen to the reaction of your own body and that of your partner. The biggest turn-on is seeing your partner respond excitedly to your touch."

I wasn't sure if she was talking more about what *she* was feeling at this precise moment, or referring to what we were experiencing. It must have been even more exciting for her watching two sexy women touching their naked bodies only a few feet in front of her. With her special sex toy working its wonders underneath her business suit, I imagined she'd have experienced multiple climaxes facilitating these sessions.

"Don't forget to communicate how you feel," she said. "Tell your partner what she's doing to you right now."

"I'm so excited watching Jade touch herself," Haley said. "I never thought a woman could look this sexy and beautiful before. The feelings inside are even more intense than last time–"

"And *you*, Jade?" Hannah said. "How is your body responding seeing Haley get excited watching you?"

"Oh my God," I groaned. "I want her so bad. I want to touch her and taste her and feel her trembling in my arms."

"Soon enough," Hannah smiled. "For now, I just want you both to learn how to satisfy one another at a distance without the added pressure of direct engagement. Focus on what you're feeling, and surrender to the pleasure engulfing your bodies. As before, feel free to experiment with different forms of stimulation. You can begin learning from one another even before you come together."

I spread my legs further apart and inserted two fingers from my other hand into my hole as I began to rub my clit more quickly.

"Mmm, yes," I panted. "You're so beautiful, Haley. I'm imagining you touching me..."

"Yes, Jade," Haley said. "I want to touch you and feel your wetness. You're making me so hot right now."

Haley mimicked my technique, awkwardly inserting the middle finger of her left hand into her slit while she pumped it in and out as she began jilling herself more rapidly. Our hips began to slowly lift off our divans and our mouths opened in pleasure as we moved inexorably closer to orgasm.

"Yes, baby," I purred. "I want to watch you let it go. Imagine me sucking your jewel as you come in my mouth–"

"Oh God," Haley squealed as she arched her hips higher in the air. "It's *coming*! Suck my pussy, Jade!"

Suddenly, Haley fell back onto the surface of the divan and she hunched over, jerking her body back and forth while she pressed her fingers deeper inside her pussy. Seeing her come just inches away from me was more than I could take. I suddenly flipped over on all fours and pounded my cunt as my tits wobbled excitedly over my chest. Within seconds, my orgasm washed over me like a tidal wave as I began squirting long streams in Haley's direction. While I peered at her between my legs, I saw her mouth gape wider apart as she watched me writhing uncontrollably on the chair in front of her.

I glanced over at Hannah for a moment and saw her slumping rhythmically in her own chair as she watched the two of us cumming with our fingers deeply embedded in our pussies. I smiled, knowing she had her *own* special finger stimulating her G-spot as she surrendered to an entirely different kind of lover.

4
____

After we all came down from our highs at Hannah's therapy session, she asked Haley and me if we were ready to proceed to the next stage in our intimacy journey. Knowing this meant we'd be allowed to touch each other, we both quickly agreed, but since we'd used up all the allotted time in the day's session, Hannah scheduled our next meeting for the following week. When we parted, Haley and I kissed each other on the cheek, but that was enough to keep me going until we met next time.

In the intervening week, I ran through all kinds of scenarios imagining how I'd like to touch and caress her. It was kind of fun not using any toys for a change, since I knew those would be off base during our next encounter. Hannah didn't want any artificial stimulation getting in the way of Haley learning to enjoy sex in the natural manner. That was easy for *her* to say, I thought, remembering how she'd responded watching Haley and me writhing on our divans while she let her special sex toy do all the work for her. But I knew she was right, and as I lay on my sofa dreaming of all the ways I could stimulate Haley, I came many times remembering what she'd said to me when she experienced her first orgasm in the presence of another woman.

This time, I thought, *she won't need to pretend that I'm touching her when she comes next to me.*

On the day of our next scheduled session, we arrived at Hannah's office a few minutes early, which gave her a chance to prep us and set the ground rules. The most important thing, she said, was to go slow and make sure our partner felt comfortable before pushing any further.

I looked around her office and noticed that the two settees had been pushed to the side, and I looked at her inquisitively.

"Where did you want us to relax?" I asked.

Hannah smiled as she led us into another room with a four-poster bed. The drapes had been pulled and a series of candles were lit around the room to set the mood. I could smell a hint of lemongrass from some burning incense on the night table, and I nodded at Hannah's preparation.

"I thought you might like something a little more comfortable to relax on this time," she said. "Plus, I suspect you'll need a little more room to maneuver as you begin to explore each other's bodies. I wanted to make sure you felt as cozy as possible before proceeding to the next step. Why don't you give it a try and see what you think?"

I strolled up to the bed and ran my fingers over the linens. The high thread count made the bedding feel like silk, and I got goosebumps imagining what it would feel like to lie next to Haley on the sumptuous surface.

"What do you think, Haley?" I said. "Do you think this will be suitable for our purposes?"

Haley stepped forward and ran her hands over the sheets, then turned toward Hannah and smiled.

"It feels like I'm in a five-star hotel," she said. "I've never experienced anything so luxurious in my entire life."

"I wanted you to feel completely relaxed in preparation for the next step in your journey of sexual awakening."

"What about *you*?" Haley asked. "Where will you be while Jade and I are resting on the bed?"

Hannah turned to a reclining chair resting in the corner of the room.

"I'll be sitting in the shadows not too far away. I want there to be minimum distraction while you and Jade explore each other's bodies."

"So you'll be with us for the remainder of the session then?"

"If that's what you prefer."

"You were very helpful last time," Haley nodded. "Plus, it somehow seems more erotic knowing you'll be watching us."

Hannah paused as she peered at the two of us with a sly smile.

"I'll try to be less involved this time while I give each of you a chance to experiment with what turns you on. But I assure you that I'll be enjoying the process almost as much as you will."

She walked to the other side of the room and lay down in her chair, crossing her legs.

"To get you in the mood, sometimes it can be more exciting to let your partner take your clothes off before you lie down. Who'd like to begin?"

Haley and I peered at one another, and a blush fell over her cheeks. It was obvious that she wanted me to make the first move, which was fine with me since I'd been undressing her with my eyes from the moment we came in the door. She'd chosen to wear a more formal outfit today, with a collared blouse, wool pants, and suede loafers. Whether she was trying to mimic me or she was trying to project the image of more sophisticated woman, was unclear. Either way, I liked the look, and I felt my heart beating faster as I imagined unbuttoning her blouse.

I stepped forward and reached out my hand to her, and she met mine with her opposite hand, squeezing my fingers gently. I tilted my head down, and she closed her eyes, anticipating my kiss. Pausing an inch from her mouth, I felt her cool breath on my skin, and my pussy twitched when I realized I was about to touch her intimately for the first time.

When our lips touched, she puckered them like they used to in old-time movies. I smiled, realizing that this might have been the first romantic contact she'd ever experienced and that she still hadn't learned the art of erotic kissing. I lifted my hand and cupped her face as I moved closer, pressing my body against hers. She unconsciously tilted her pelvis, pressing her hips against mine. I parted my mouth and nibbled her flesh, feeling the fullness of her lips.

She sighed as we pressed our breasts together, and I circled my arm around her, caressing the indentation of her lower back. I was dying to plunge my tongue into her, but I remembered Hannah's admonition about going slowly, and instead I turned around and sat down on the bed with my knees straddling her hips. While Haley peered down at me, I began to loosen the buttons of her blouse from the top. As I began to spread the panels apart, I smiled when I noticed that she was wearing a lacy bra like the one I'd worn at our last session.

I leaned in and kissed her exposed belly with my moist lips, reaching up to cup her breasts as I squeezed them gently. She began to moan and reached behind my head to run her fingers through my hair. I'd almost forgotten how to properly make love a woman with all my recent escapades, and suddenly I was happy that I'd agree to participate in Hannah's guided session.

Maybe I'd needed this as much as Haley did.

As she pulled my head tighter against her belly, I reached behind her and unfastened the clasp at the back of her bra, pulling it gently over her shoulders. Her brassiere fell below her breasts, and I lifted myself up, licking her pointy tips. Her nipples were hard and warm, and as I sucked them into my mouth one at a time, she gasped, pulling my head harder against her body. As I began to roll my tongue over her tips, I moved my hands to the front of her chest and squeezed her breasts more tightly. They felt full and firm in my palms, and for the first time since I'd entered the office, I became conscious of the warm feeling in my pussy. My juices had been flowing for some time now, and the feeling of wetness between my legs made my nipples harden.

Haley was running her fingers through my hair more wildly now, and I took this to mean that she was ready for me to take it to the next step. I traced my hands down the front of her belly, unclasping the button at the top of her pants, then I slowly pulled the zipper down to reveal a pair of black lace panties. Seeing her wearing sexy lingerie got me even more turned on, and I slipped my fingers over the waist of her pants and began to pull them down over her hips.

My heart pounded as I felt them tighten up when they reached the widest part of her hips, realizing just how curvy and tight her ass must have been. As I pulled them further down her thighs, Haley lifted her feet and kicked off her loafers, stepping out of her jeans. I pulled her blouse off her back, and her brassiere fell softly onto the floor. Now she stood inches away from me, almost naked and quivering in excitement.

Hannah must have sensed Haley's trepidation, as I heard her shift in her chair for the first time and clear her throat.

"Sometimes it's even more erotic to have your partner remove her clothes while you *watch*," she said. "Would you like to undress Jade yourself Haley, or watch her do so herself?"

"I've been dreaming of seeing her naked again this whole week," Haley said. "But I'm not as experienced as Jade in the art of undressing another woman..."

Taking Haley's cue, I stood up off the bed and stepped back a few paces to give her a chance to take in my full figure. I smiled at her as I began to slowly unbutton my blouse. I'd decided to go braless for today's session, and as it became apparent to Haley that I was naked under my shirt, I saw her eyes widening in excitement. After I unclasped the fourth button, I let the silky fabric fall on top of my breasts while I breathed in and out deeply. As my nipples began to harden, pressing against the soft fabric, Haley's lips begin to separate.

I teased her for a moment longer, bringing my hands together and pushing my tits closer together. She panted looking at my cleavage, and I felt my pussy getting wetter seeing her rising excitement. When I undid the last button and threw my blouse on the bed beside me, I watched the flickering light casting sexy shadows over Haley's mounds. I wanted to step forward and trib her pointed nipples with my own, but I reminded myself that this session was all about her. The more slowly I could build her desire, the more I knew she'd enjoy the moment when we finally came together.

Damn, I thought. It had been a long time since I'd been

this patient in seducing another woman. Apparently I needed Hannah's guided lessons just as much as Haley.

As we stood facing each other in the hypnotic shadows, Haley glanced down my midsection and a small curl formed on the side of her lips. For the same reason she'd chosen to dress more maturely, I'd chosen to wear jeans so she'd feel more comfortable seeing me as a peer. But the problem with the tight jeans was that they revealed the widening wet spot between my legs far more easily than when I wore my skirt.

"It looks like you're getting just as excited as me," Haley smiled, locking her eyes on my dark stain.

"Sorry," I shrugged. "I guess I lubricate a little more easily than most women."

"Mmm, I like that," Haley purred. "I can't wait to feel you. I'm beginning to get wet too."

I glanced down at Haley's legs and saw the shimmering slickness on the inside of her thighs.

"Perhaps it's time for the two of you to get more comfortable on the bed," Hannah interrupted from the darkness.

I'd almost forgotten she was there, but far from finding her intrusions irritating, I was glad she knew when we needed a little prompt. I slipped off my jeans, then lay down on the bed with my arm cocked sexily against the side of my head in a come-hither look to Haley. She didn't hesitate to join me on the other side of the bed, and we quickly melted into each other's arms. As I felt her press her body against mine, I kissed her with an open mouth, and this time she parted her lips and allowed my tongue to probe her cavity. Our breasts mashed together, and as we intertwined our legs, we both began to moan passionately. I pulled my leg up, pressing it against her pussy, and she responded by grinding her hips against my thigh.

By now, she'd joined me in thrusting her tongue into my

mouth, and as we writhed together on the bed, I grabbed her ass and pulled her closer. The passion with which she was tongue-fucking me made me think she was ready for different kind of tongue lashing, and after a few minutes I disengaged and began nibbling my way down the front of her body. The only sound I could hear from the other sound of the room now was the soft rusting of Hannah shifting in her chair and the occasional soft sigh. I wondered if Haley sensed how much she was enjoying herself watching us, but at this point my only concern was satisfying the pretty girl lying beside me.

As I nibbled on Haley's teats and swirled my tongue over her areolas, she arched her back and pressed herself more firmly against me. It was apparent to me that she'd lost all of her inhibitions about being with another woman, and I hummed my approval as her body responded to my touch. I traced the little indentation running down the center of her tummy with my tongue, and her stomach quivered the closer I got to her private area as she began to roll her hips in anticipation of my touch.

When I reached her panties, I pulled them over her hips while she lifted her ass off the bed. Her bush felt as soft as fur and I rolled my cheeks over it, reveling in it's sexy scent and plush thickness. Beads of lubrication rested on her muff like morning dew on a spider web, and I paused to suck them into my mouth, tasting her sweet honey.

The further down I lowered myself, the further she spread her legs apart, until my shoulders were comfortably nestled between her legs. For a moment, I paused with my head cocked above her clit as I closed my eyes and inhaled her sweet, perfumy scent. After a few moments, she began to shimmy her hips impatiently, eager to feel my touch in her special place. Instead, I dribbled some saliva out of my mouth and let it fall on top of her inflamed jewel. When she felt the unexpected moisture on her button, she groaned and lifted her hips closer to my face.

"Oh God, Jade," she whined. "You're driving me crazy. I want to feel your touch so bad. Take me into your mouth like you said you would last time. Suck my pussy with your pretty mouth."

Her dirty talk just turned me on all the more, and I lowered my head to encircle her burning clit.

"Oh God–Oh God," Haley panted. "That feels so good. Lick my little man with your lips and make me feel like you did when I watched you last time."

Little man, I chuckled to myself. I hadn't heard that expression used by a woman before to describe her clit, and I wondered if this was a euphemism her parents had used when she was younger. But it didn't matter to me–I was just thrilled that she was expressing her desire for me and telling me how much I was turning her on.

As I hummed in delight, I began circling her button with the tip of my tongue, and she began groaning more loudly. While I mixed up my technique between sucking and licking her pearl, she placed her hands behind my head once again and pulled me harder into her crotch. As her breathing began to get more ragged and accelerated, I knew that she was getting close to the point of no return. I was tempted to pull back for a few seconds to prolong her torment, but then I realized there'd be plenty more time to tease and play with her after she released her pent-up sexual tension. She began to lift her hips off the bed as her body became rigid in a tight lock, and I slipped my fingers inside her and began to stroke her tenting G-spot.

"Oh God, Jade," she hissed. "Don't stop. I'm going to cum. *Yes!*" she grunted. "I'm cumming in your mouth!"

Suddenly, I felt the walls of her pussy clamping down on my fingers in rhythmic contractions as she humped her hips against my face while holding me tightly against her. I paused for a moment to feel her body spasming as I peered up and watched her pretty face contorting into paroxysms of pleasure. After what seemed like a full minute of tensing her body in a prolonged and powerful orgasm, she finally dropped her hips down onto the bed, panting loudly to catch her breath.

With the room suddenly quiet, I heard gentle squeaks coming from the other side of the room as Hannah shifted rhythmically in her chair. It was obvious to both of us what was going on in the dark, and we smiled at one another as I pulled myself back up to look into Haley's steamy eyes.

"That was beautiful, Jade," she sighed. "Thank you for making me feel like a woman for the first time in my life. I can't believe how skilled a lover you are. I'm afraid that I'll never be able to meet your expectations–"

"Remember that there are no expectations or targets in this first direct encounter between the two of you," Hannah breathed deeply, collecting herself. "Jade–why don't you show Haley how she can satisfy you. Sometimes it's more fun for the *receiver* to take the lead."

I knew immediately what Hannah meant, and as I lifted myself up off the bed, I looked into Haley's eyes and nodded.

"Why don't you lie there for a little longer and let me do most of the work?" I said.

I raised myself up on all fours and straddled her face with my knees on either side of her head, and she looked up at me with wide eyes and smiled. As I ran my fingers gently through her silky hair, I began to lower myself until my dripping pussy hovered inches over her pouty lips. She flicked her tongue out awkwardly trying to bat my clit, and I cupped her cheeks, lowering myself a little further until my nub pressed against her lips.

"Just open your mouth a little bit and nibble on me for a moment," I said. "Sometimes when you're making love to a woman, less is more. Let me ease into it while I watch your pretty face."

Haley did as she was told, and as she sucked my hard nub into her mouth, I closed my eyes and groaned.

"Yes, baby," I purred. "Just like that. Suck my button and roll it around in your mouth. I like the feeling of your mouth on my body."

As Haley began to roll her tongue over my bulb in a similar manner to the way I'd kissed her earlier, I smiled. She was a quick study, and I felt myself growing closer to her with every passing moment.

"Yes, Haley," I encouraged her. "Just like that. Feel my hard clit in your mouth. I'm making love to your mouth while I watch you. I'm going to cum for you soon."

Haley's head nodded excitedly, and her eyes began to widen as I pressed my pussy harder down onto her face. I could feel the passion rising within me but I didn't want to drown her in another torrent if I came too hard, so as my orgasm began to take hold of me, I lifted my hips and pointed my pussy over her tits while I squirted my juices all over her heaving chest. As she peered down at me between my legs, I saw her face twist into another silent orgasm. Apparently, I'd excited her so much with my waterworks that she hadn't needed any direct stimulation to come once again.

As we both groaned and shook our bodies together on the bed, I heard the sound of gentle sloshing coming from the direction of Hannah's chair. I peered over at her and noticed that her pants were unbuttoned while she rubbed her hands sensuously over her naked mound.

"That was very good, ladies," she sighed. "You're making excellent progress. It's time for the last step in your pair bonding. Now I want you to touch each other at the same time and experience the joy of coming together. Jade, I'm guessing you have a bit more experience in this area."

"Perhaps just a little," I smiled, as I shimmied my hips over Haley's slippery torso toward her quivering pussy. I paused for a moment when I reached her bush once again and tilted my pelvis back and forth over top of her bush, feeling the soft hairs tickling my clit and wet opening.

"Would you like me to make love to you now, Haley?" I purred.

"Isn't that what we've been doing all this time?" she said.

"Not quite *this* way," I smiled. "I think you might find this brings us even closer together and feels even more amazing. Lift your knees up higher and spread your legs for me."

Haley looked at me confused for a moment, and I nodded reassuringly. When she pulled her knees almost up to her chest, I pushed her thighs apart and peered at her inflamed gland, poking its head out of its hood. I kneeled over top of her and slowly lowered my body until the bottom of our thighs rested on one another. Her eyes widened when she realized what I intended to do, and a sly smile formed on my mouth as our clits touched for the first time. As I began to grind our hips together providing direct stimulation to our most sensitive areas, she threw her head back and groaned . I didn't know if she'd even conceived of two women touching themselves this way, but the look of pleasure on her face indicated that she was quickly losing herself in the process.

As I shifted my weight forward and back, stroking her

hard clit and rubbing our sopping pussies together, she began to whimper and toss her head from side to side. Seeing her enjoying the tribbing action so much just made me want to fuck her harder. I transferred more of my weight onto her thighs, and she began to rock her hips in concert with mine. The feeling of our nubs rolling over one another as our slits smacked against one another was the most exciting feeling either one of us had experienced. Before long, she began moaning more urgently, and I saw a flush begin to spread over her chest as her nipples contracted even more firmly.

"Yes, Haley," I groaned, seeing the look of ecstasy roll over her face. "Let it go baby. Let me feel you cum with me while I make love to you."

"Yes, Jade," Haley grunted. "I feel it coming. I'm going to cum so hard against your pussy. Fuck me harder."

That was all I needed to hear as I pressed my hips harder down onto her vulva and began humping her more forcefully. When I heard her pussy begin to make sexy gassy sounds, I knew she was cumming again, but this time I stayed connected to her while my own orgasm took hold of me. The sound of my juices spraying onto her gaping hole as she moaned in euphoria was the sexiest thing I'd ever heard. As we came together listening to the sound of our pussies spasming in the height of ecstasy, I leaned forward and kissed her passionately. Haley had come a long way since her first awkward guided session with Hannah, and as our pussies continued twitching against one another, we both sighed in contentment.

Soon after, we heard Hannah moaning softly in her chair, and we turned our heads to see that she'd pulled her pants down all the way and was ramming her long dildo in and out of her pussy.

"I'd have to say you've both graduated with flying colors," she panted as her body jerked softly in her chair.

Haley and I looked at each for a moment with the same thought, nodding our heads in Hannah's direction.

"I think maybe Hannah needs a little therapy session of her *own* now," I smiled.

There's more than one way to break the boredom when the power goes out...

Everybody's an exhibitionist in disguise...

Spying on the neighbors just got a lot more interesting...

Everything's sexier in the dark...

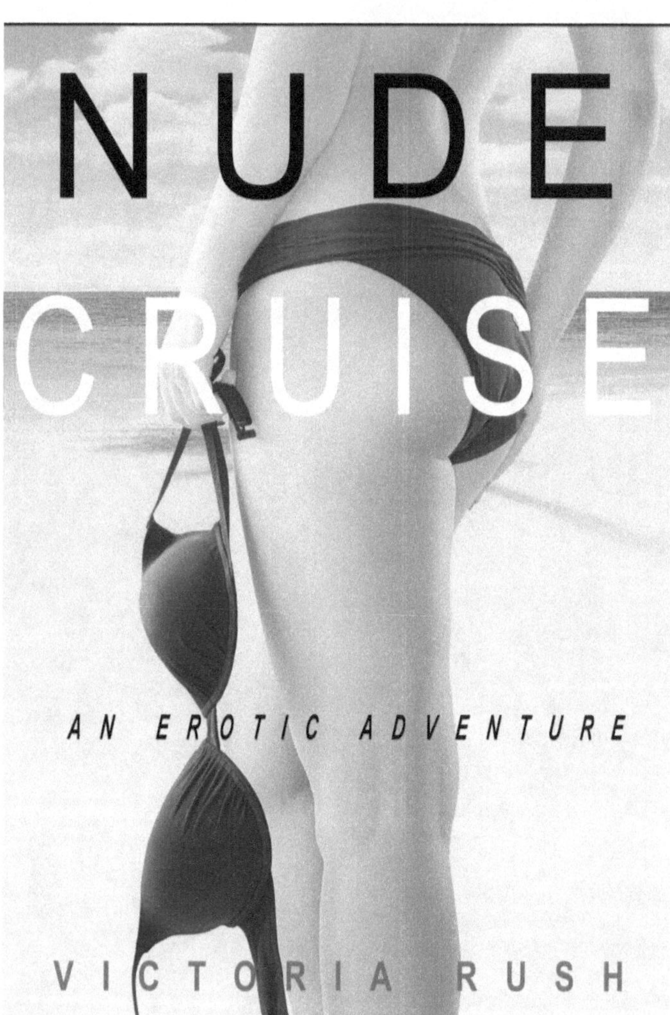

Some people get wet on a cruise for different reasons...

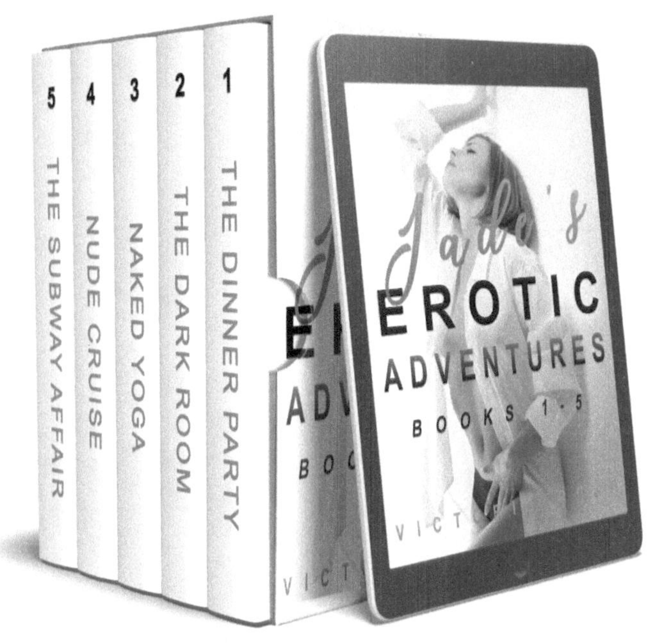

Books 1 -5 in the bestselling series - 60% off

THE DINNER PARTY - PREVIEW
FINGER FOOD

S ometime later, I heard a soft tap on my bedroom door. Not wanting to remove myself just yet from my cocoon of luxury, I called out to answer.

"Yes?"

"It's time for your massage," a woman's voice replied.

"Just one minute please."

I reluctantly stepped out of the bath and quickly toweled myself dry. I wrapped a large bath sheet around me, re-donned my mask, then opened the bedroom door.

A petite young Asian girl greeted me, wearing a kimono similar to mine and a crimson masquerade mask.

Apparently not everybody who works here always walks around stark naked.

The girl was utterly breathtaking. Long jet-black hair cascaded over high cheekbones past pouty lips, her delicate collarbones peeking from the top of her kimono. I could see her breasts and hips outlined by the tightly-wrapped kimono and suddenly wished that she too had come to my boudoir naked.

"My name is Jasmine," she said. "I'm your personal

masseuse and esthetician. Are you ready for your final preparation?

Just the thought of this beauty laying her tender hands on me sent a shiver down my spine.

"Definitely. Please come in. How would you like me to prepare?"

"Come with me, please."

Jasmine led me into the bathroom, where she nonchalantly removed her kimono and hung it behind the bathroom door.

Oh my God.

I didn't think anyone in this place could get more beautiful or sensuous. Jasmine had perfectly shaped B-cup breasts with a thin indentation running down the center of her perfectly toned stomach. Like everyone else in this place, her pubis was utterly bald and flawless. She barely looked eighteen and I was just about to ask her age, but she spoke first.

"If you'd like to remove your towel and lay face down on the table, we can get started. May I call you Jade?"

There was something about her confident manner and tone that belied her youthful appearance. I had no inhibitions whatsoever about displaying myself unclothed to this stranger.

"Yes, thank you, Jasmine." I unhooked my bath sheet and threw it against the side of the tub.

"Would you like me to drape your backside?" Jasmine asked.

"That won't be necessary," I quickly answered.

Jasmine walked over to the vanity counter and picked up two small bottles of oil resting under an orange radiant lamp. She brought them back to the massage table, opened one, and poured the oil into one cupped hand then rubbed her hands together. The scent of lavender wafted toward my nose.

I closed my eyes in anticipation of her touch. I'd had massages before, but nothing as sensuous and stimulating as this. When her hands touched the small of my back, I jerked reflexively from the sexual tension. My heart was beating a hundred miles an hour as I felt the blood coursing through my veins.

Jasmine must have sensed my nervous tension and began pressing her fingers more firmly into my back as she moved them slowly up each side of my spine. The warm oil allowed her hands to glide effortlessly across my skin. She used every surface of her hands to massage my muscles, expertly kneading my skin with her fingers and palm.

I began to relax as my muscles softened and surrendered to her touch. She sensuously massaged every part of my back, shoulders, and neck, applying just the right amount of pressure. Periodically, she would pour more warm oil on my lower back, dipping her hands in it to replenish the silky lubrication against my pliant skin.

Just as the sexual tension began to subside from the utter relaxation of the massage, Jasmine moved her hands down to my buttocks and began to caress them in soft circular motions. My glutes contracted involuntarily and I unconsciously pressed my mound into the firm padding of the table. Suddenly I was quickly reminded that a gorgeous young woman was caressing my naked body. She cupped each buttock between her hands as she massaged my ass tantalizingly, her little finger sliding slowly into the cleft just above my anus.

Periodically, I'd partially open one of my eyes with my head turned in her direction to look at her gorgeous body. My head was at the same level as her midsection, and my mouth watered as I watched her stomach muscles flex and her hips undulate with each movement of her hands. At times her pussy was almost right beside me and I wanted to reach out and run my own fingers up her soft legs.

I was in total heaven and getting wetter by the moment. Just when I thought I couldn't stand it anymore, she suddenly moved her hands down to my feet and began massaging her thumbs into my soles.

I'd always loved having my feet massaged, but nobody did it like Jasmine. She cradled my foot and used every part of her hands to massage and knead every surface from my heel to my toes. I didn't want her to stop, but there were other parts of my body that were screaming for attention.

As if reading my thoughts, she began moving her hands up toward my calf, using her thumbs to spread the muscle apart. She lingered almost as long on my calf as she had on my foot, rolling the ball of my calf between both of her hands, sliding her slick hands up and down erotically. I couldn't help imagining how she might use those same hands to massage a man's erect cock in a similar manner. My mind wandered again to what pleasures lay in wait for me over dinner.

After shifting her hands to my right leg and giving my other foot and calf similar attention, she placed each hand just behind my knees and began to slowly move them up towards my buttocks. Her thumbs pressed against my inner thighs as she glided tantalizingly close to my apex.

I rolled my legs outward in an invitation to move closer. My legs were parted enough that I was sure she could see my vulva from her vantage point behind me. In my highly aroused state, my lips were engorged and spread apart, revealing my moist and quivering opening.

But as much as I desperately wanted her to, Jasmine

never touched me there. She repeatedly slid her hands right up to the edge of my slit, pressing and rotating her thumbs on the fleshy meat of my upper thighs just below my aching pussy. I suppose this was part of her master plan—to tease me mercilessly and inflame my passions so I'd be ready for just about anything at the main event.

It was certainly working. After thirty minutes of Jasmine's ministrations, I was grinding my pussy into the table trying desperately to give my clit some needed direct stimulation.

Just when I thought I couldn't be teased any more tantalizingly, Jasmine opened one of the bottles of warm oil and poured it directly into the crack of my ass. She paused as the fluid flowed down and directly over my parted lips. I almost came from the gentle movement of the warm liquid as it trickled across the folds of my labia, channeled toward the junction where they joined together at my clit. I shuddered in pleasure at the feeling, even if it was only the subtlest of touch.

Jasmine suddenly interrupted my thoughts.

"Would you like to turn over now?"

It was the first time she had spoken directly to me since the massage started, and it surprised me in my catatonic, pre-orgasmic state. I practically flipped over like a fish out of water and spread my legs expectantly. Finally, I'd get some relief. Surely, she couldn't leave me hanging like this.

"It's time for your final grooming," she said. "I'll need you to part your legs a bit further to provide full access."

Grooming? I knew this was part of the process, but somehow it didn't seem fair to transition at this precise moment. At least I'd be able to stay on the comfortable massage table instead of the clinical vinyl chairs used by my regular esthetician.

Jasmine walked over to another cabinet by the makeup table and withdrew a leather bag from one of the drawers, then brought it back to the table. She reached into the bag and pulled out a cordless hair trimmer.

"Do you have a preference regarding your appearance?" she asked. "Do you prefer natural, neatly trimmed, or bare?"

I knew she was referring to my pubic hair, which I generally kept neatly trimmed. I'd always thought going fully bald was unnatural and unseemly, catering to men's prurient fantasies of fucking young schoolgirls. But in this situation, it seemed entirely appropriate, like I was stripping away all my camouflage and armor.

If tonight was all about being watched, I might as well bare myself in every sense of the word and truly let my inhibitions go. I began to fantasize about rubbing my bare pussy against Jasmine's while she poured warm oil between us. The more work she had to do on me, the more chance I'd have to make this last and hopefully get off.

I didn't hesitate. "Bare, thank you."

"As you wish," she said. "I'll remove the long hairs first with the trimmer, then shave you smooth with a razor."

No waxing? This was different. I was relieved to not have to bear the painful and violent trial of having my hairs ripped out en masse. Although shaving down there was always a scary proposition, I felt safe in the capable and practiced hands of this beautiful esthetician.

Jasmine nodded, then flipped a switch on the trimmer. The device buzzed softly as she placed it gently on my mound. I had only a light dusting of fur and it didn't take long for her to remove it with a few short strokes over my pubis. I shuddered as the vibrations penetrated deep into my core. If she had placed the flat head on my clitoris, I would have popped off in a millisecond. Instead, she turned the trimmer face-down and gently swiped the vibrating teeth against the sides of my vulva, sensuously separating my labia with her hands as she moved the device between my legs to trim the hairs on the inside and outside of my labia.

It was an insanely titillating feeling, but just clinical enough to bring me down from my plateau and shift my focus. My mind wandered to the upcoming feast, and I contemplated what surprises lay in wait at the main event. The hostesses had suggested there would be 'contact' of some sort during the meal, and I was intrigued exactly who and how it would be administered. The idea of being fully bald, cleansed, and thoroughly stimulated going into the event was an incredible rush.

Jasmine continued with the trimmer all the way down my perineum to my anus, barely touching me with the trimmer so as not to pinch any delicate tissues. Apparently there were no parts of my erogenous zone that would remain untouched, now—and perhaps later.

She turned off the trimmer and placed it at the foot of the table. Then she took a bottle of gel from the bag and spread the gel on her hands. Using both hands, she spread it gently between my legs, starting on my mound all the way down to my rosebud.

My body almost levitated above the table as Jasmine finally laid her hands directly on my clitoris. The gel had a mild stinging quality that added to the stimulating sensation. If this was meant to excite my follicles in preparation for the shave, it wasn't the only feature of my anatomy that it made erect. I could feel the hood of my clitoris retract as my button filled with blood and began to push outward. Suddenly, I was fully stimulated again and lusting for Jasmine's touch. I fantasized about her bending down and taking my swollen nub between her puffy lips and letting me come in her mouth.

Unfortunately, my satisfaction would have to wait a little longer. Instead, Jasmine reached into her bag and pulled out a straight-edge razor. In anyone else's hands, it might look threatening, especially in my prostrated and vulnerable position. But something about the way she delicately and sensuously opened the jackknifed tool instantly evaporated my fears. I could see how this type of razor would in fact give her better control safely cutting my stubs instead of the usual ladies plastic razor.

With her right hand, Jasmine gently laid the razor on its flat edge at the top of my mound, while she gently pulled my skin upwards with her other hand. Then she slowly turned the sharp edge perpendicular to my skin and began softly scraping the razor downwards. I could hear the bristling sound as the razor edge removed my nubs right down to the follicles. She repeated the pattern in one inch wide swipes on one side then the other of my pubis, being ever-so-careful to stop just where my clitoris lay quivering in a mixture of fear and excitement. There was something about the utter vulnerability of the procedure that made it the most erotic experience I'd ever had.

Jasmine used the same deft touch as she moved down my vulva and perineum, scraping the vestiges of stray hairs away with gentle swipes of the long blade, while sensuously separating my folds and flesh with her other hand. She took extra time and care around my anus and clit, using the gentlest and slowest motion I've ever felt someone apply to my body. The combination of fright and titillation as she probed my most sensitive body parts created a river of sensuous fluids running down my vulva. By this time, no shaving gel was necessary to provide a smooth gliding surface for the knife.

When she was finished, Jasmine retrieved a fresh wash towel from beside the sink and held it under the warm water faucet then twisted the excess water into the basin. She returned to the table and placed it over my splayed legs then gently cleansed the excess moisture and remaining shaving gel with gentle massaging movements of her hands. The warm, moist towel felt exquisite against my newly shaved skin. Jasmine's hands now felt comforting between my legs rather than erotic.

She had taken me on an incredibly sensuous erotic arc, right to the edge of ecstasy and back, to a quiet relaxed place. I exhaled fully and completely for the first time in almost an hour.

Jasmine removed the towel from between my legs and held up a large hand mirror at a forty-five degree angle toward me.

"What do you think?" she asked.

I tilted my head up and studied her masterpiece. Far from the usual red and swollen vulva that I typically experienced after the violent waxing with my regular esthetician, I'd never seen my pussy look so beautiful. Utterly bereft of any hair, my entire perineum from my pubic mound to my anus was totally bald, pink—and gorgeous. I just stared at my beautiful pussy, utterly transfixed by the transformation.

"You have to *feel* it to really appreciate how beautiful you are, Jade," Jasmine purred.

I moved my right hand down, running my fingers along the edges of my pussy. I gasped from a feeling I'd never felt before. It felt smooth as silk: no bumps or blemishes or cuts or bruises. It was almost as if I was feeling somebody else— somebody I'd never felt before. I couldn't stop my left hand joining the other in rubbing and caressing my sensitive organs.

Jasmine lowered the mirror and smiled at me as I felt the moisture begin to accumulate between my legs again.

"It's almost time for your dinner appointment," she said. "Why don't you save the best for last? I think you'll find plenty of ways to satisfy your appetite over the next couple of hours."

She lifted my kimono from the hook at the edge of the bathtub and held it open for me.

"I'll escort you downstairs now if you're ready. All you need to bring is your kimono and slippers—and your mask of course."

I sat up slowly and stepped off the massage table. Turning around, I held my arms out as Jasmine lifted one arm of the silk robe onto me then the other. Then she turned around to face me, wrapped the silk tie around me, and tied a single bow over my belly button. She retrieved my matching silk slippers and knelt down on one knee to gently lift my feet one at a time and place them softly inside. It took every ounce of my power not to grab her head and pull it into my pulsating pussy.

Jasmine stood up gracefully and smiled into my eyes.

"If you'll follow me, I'll escort you now to the fantasy feast."

She didn't bother putting her own robe on. Her tight little ass barely jiggled as she stepped smartly ahead of me. I wasn't sure if I'd have a chance to feel Jasmine's touch again before the evening was over, but for now I was in total bliss ogling her petite, curvaceous figure from behind...

Read More

ABOUT THE AUTHOR

If you would like to receive notification of new book(s) in Jade's Erotic Adventures, follow me at http://bookbub.com/authors/victoria-rush.

If you have a moment, please post a brief review on my Amazon book page at viewbook.at/thetherapist . Even just a couple of sentences will help other readers find and enjoy this book as much as you hopefully did.

Follow, share, like, and comment at:

www.facebook.com/authorvictoriarush
www.pinterest.com/authorvictoriarush
www.twitter.com/authorvictoriarush
authorvictoriarush@outlook.com

Hope to see you again soon!

www.ingramcontent.com/pod-product-compliance
Lightning Source LLC
Chambersburg PA
CBHW030822200726
48288CB00004B/1341